THOMAS & FRIENDS

KING OF THE RAILWAY

Illustrated by Tommy Stubbs

 A GOLDEN BOOK • NEW YORK

Thomas the Tank Engine & Friends™

CREATED BY BRITT ALLCROFT

Based on The Railway Series by The Reverend W Awdry.
© 2013 Gullane (Thomas) LLC.
Thomas the Tank Engine & Friends and Thomas & Friends are trademarks of Gullane (Thomas) Limited.
HIT and the HIT Entertainment logo are trademarks of HIT Entertainment Limited.
All rights reserved. Published in the United States by Golden Books, an imprint of Random House
Children's Books, a division of Random House, Inc., 1745 Broadway, New York, NY 10019, and in Canada
by Random House of Canada Limited, Toronto. Golden Books, A Golden Book, A Little Golden Book,
the G colophon, and the distinctive gold spine are registered trademarks of Random House, Inc.
ISBN 978-0-449-81537-3
randomhouse.com/kids
www.thomasandfriends.com
Printed in the United States of America
10 9 8 7 6 5 4 3
Random House Children's Books supports the First Amendment and celebrates the right to read.

CALGARY PUBLIC LIBRARY
MAR 2018

One morning, Thomas and Percy were shunting trucks at Brendam Docks. Suddenly, a truck bashed into Percy's buffer and tipped over. A crate fell out and split open.

"Thomas, look!" peeped Percy. "There's a robot!"

"That's not a robot," grumbled Cranky. "It's a suit of armor."

"Cranky's right," said Sir Topham Hatt.
"Once, the Island of Sodor was ruled by
kings and knights. The greatest king was the
beloved King Godred. He wore a golden crown.
But the crown went missing long ago!"

An earl was visiting the island. Thomas
delivered the crate to him. There he met
Millie, the earl's Narrow Gauge engine.

"I run the estate railway for the earl," Millie
peeped happily.

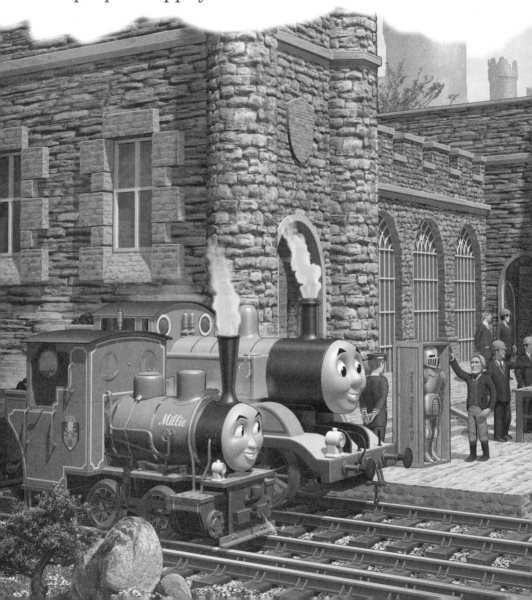

"I wish I had King Godred's golden crown," said the earl. "Then my plan would be complete."

Thomas' friend Jack the Digger was also working at the estate.

"I'm helping the earl restore the castle," puffed Jack.

"So *that's* his plan!" whistled Thomas.

Thomas, Percy, and James spent the day happily shunting containers . . . until Thomas came upon a flatbed with a large crate on it. The earl said it was a special delivery for the Steamworks.

At the Steamworks, a gantry crane lifted the crate and revealed an old engine named Stephen. His wood was worn, and he had rust holes in his boiler.

"Surprise!" the old engine peeped.

Victor said he'd have Stephen fixed up in no time.

"I have a special job for Stephen," said the earl. "But it's best not to say anything yet."

"I won't," peeped Thomas. "I promise."

Victor worked quickly. Soon Stephen's funnel was straightened and his boiler was fixed. With a fresh coat of paint, he was good as new.

As Thomas rolled away to work, he noticed
that Stephen looked sad.

Thomas told Stephen that the earl had a
special job for him. Stephen was very excited.

Stephen wondered what his special job would be. Victor didn't know, so Stephen rolled down to Brendam Docks.

"There's no work here for an old engine like you," Cranky said.

Stephen wound his way up to the quarry.
"I'm looking for my new job," Stephen said.
"We can always use help," Luke peeped.
But each truck Stephen tried to pull was
just too heavy.

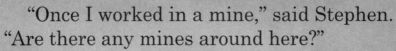

"Once I worked in a mine," said Stephen.
"Are there any mines around here?"

"There is an old mine near the castle ruins,"
said Skarloey.

Stephen found the entrance to the mine,
but it was boarded up. No one had worked
there in years.

Suddenly, some Troublesome Trucks slipped loose and roared down the hill. They were headed right toward Stephen! He had no choice but to push into the mine.

Stephen's funnel struck the roof, and rocks crashed down behind him, sealing up the entrance. He searched for a way out, but the tracks just led him in circles. He only found an old wooden crate.

Thomas and Percy searched for Stephen. Outside the old mine, Thomas saw something familiar lying on the ground. It was Stephen's funnel!

Thomas got Jack the Digger, who started hauling rocks away from the mine entrance. As soon as it was clear, Thomas raced into the dark mine. "Stephen!" he peeped.

Stephen heard Thomas coming his way.
He wanted to call out, but he was too weak.
Finally, Thomas turned a corner, and the
beam from his lamp revealed a welcome sight.

Thomas carefully pushed Stephen out of the dark mine. The earl was there to greet them.

"I found something in the mine," Stephen said. "There's a big wooden chest."

The next day, the earl revealed what was in the crate. It was the king's golden crown! "It is all thanks to Stephen, our castle guide," he said.

Stephen's new funnel glittered just like the crown.